Moments

of revelation and reflection

by

Anna Hayward

Grosvenor House
Publishing Limited

This book is published by
Grosvenor House Publishing Ltd
Link House
140 The Broadway, Tolworth, Surrey, KT6 7HT.
www.grosvenorhousepublishing.co.uk

A CIP record for this book
is available from the British Library

Paperback ISBN 978-1-83615-276-7
eBook ISBN 978-1-83615-277-4

Dedication

This collection is dedicated to artists in all mediums –
if you trust yourself and your imagination,
unique creativity will thrive.

Forward

When I read Anna's stories, I am always surprised by how quickly my emotions rise to the surface. From the very first lines, I find myself completely immersed – drawn into the lives of her characters, the intricacies of their situations, the quiet or sometimes startling turns of fate.

Each story is an experience, unfolding with a rhythm that feels effortless yet deliberate. Just when I think I understand where a story is leading, Anna surprises me. The endings linger, not just because they are unexpected, but because they invite reflection. How would I feel in that moment? What might happen next? What unseen details lie just beyond the page?

That is the beauty of this collection of Moments. It is more than just a series of short stories – it is an experience, one that stays with you long after you've turned the last page. Whether you devour these stories all at once or savour them slowly, I have no doubt you will find yourself just as captivated as I was.

Enjoy the journey.

Kate Wardman

Preface

Used to writing poetry, when out and about I write short descriptions of scenes, landscapes, appealing juxtapositions of light and shade, colour and form, often in nature, and the feelings these sights and shapes invoke.

Sometime later these very short descriptions can become the starting points for stories which suggest themselves to me not as finished blueprints, but gradually and organically, they come into being as I write ... I too may not know the end of the story until it happens ... and, occasionally, be just as surprised!

The stories are often short, adding to the impression of how a single moment, and whatever it contains, can change everything. The joy for the reader is in experiencing the shift themselves, either with the character, or through a sudden realization that what one thought was so is actually quite different.

These stories do well to be read aloud to others, giving them that pleasurable feeling of being surprised and uplifted.

Acknowledgments

Great thanks must go to two loving friends: Kate Wardman, who was invaluable in finding a publisher, commenting on the text and encouraging me to submit these stories, and Joan Bain, who often and with great patience, listened to my draft ramblings!

My deepest gratitude goes to the natural world in all its great and small beauties and wildness, and to those wonderfully dedicated people who protect and care for our landscapes and habitats.

Introduction

Moments is so-called because each story is about a moment in time when something significant changes either for the main character, or for the reader.

The moments, settings, characters and time periods are all different, ranging from the 18th century to the far future. The writing is highly descriptive, creating the scenes in a short space of time with imagery which is evocative of place, and uses all the senses.

Each moment instigates an unexpected shift in consciousness, understanding or awareness. Some moments are extraordinary, but some are significant only within the psychology of the character. This is discovered through their internal dialogue, since most stories are told through the eyes and thoughts of a principal actor.

The stories often home in on the power and ineffable qualities of the natural world; not just the dramatic or stunning scenes, but the small and insignificant beauties of blades of grass, a tangle of brambles under a wild hedge, a speckled fallen leaf floating on water, how soft the new leaves of larch are in the spring. The stories contain this love and arise from a connection with the landscape of Greece in particular, and all wild places.

They also contain descriptions which notice the seemingly inconsequential, the way disparate things come together at the 'right' time; moments that transcend the mundane and become ... something other ...

Contents

Walking Widdershins

Walking widdershins round the stones, he sensed a presence. Partly distracted by the child on its red bike and the dog which came sniffing at his trousers, none the less there was something indefinable which carried him forward, urged him to move to the next large rough stone leaning into the wind, and then to the next, which seemed to bow imperiously to the bordering trees beyond the ditch.

In a shaft of light from between the heavy cumulus clouds he stopped for a moment to survey the whole circle. Gaunt and somehow anthropomorphic, the stones created an atmosphere of purpose, their shadows blending in the late afternoon light, sliding over the rim of the grass and into the darkening hollows. The boy and the dog had gone. All that remained were these old rocks and the wind flowing through the beech trees like the sea.

Looking away from the circle through the great grey trunks he could see the lights of the village as they began their nightly indication of the small lives of humans. With an impatient shrug he strode straight down the embankment into the ditch, up between the trees and down towards their warmth.

He spent the night in the pub. The Fox and Hounds, not as its name implied, was a gentle place full of the small kindnesses of a close community. Listening to the farmers sharing stories of crops and yields and sipping cold lager he could feel the tensions of the day releasing their grip, and could think again of Mary. This was where she grew up, this lovely, homely place, where the only noise in the day seemed to be the croaking of rooks in the beech trees, and the occasional tractor churning away in a distant field. She would have come here on her first dates, the only entertainment for miles, laughed in the dim lit corners where young couples came towards each other tentatively, but with longing. He gazed around the bar. Would any of these men be her relatives or friends? Would they know of her? Something stopped him asking. It had been too long and he was tired of it all. Weary of the searching and the disappointments; weary of the look in people's eyes when they saw his need and couldn't help.

After a night of oblivion on a bed which was too soft, he woke thick-headed and sore. Sore all through, really, he thought, as he contemplated the day ahead. Where now? But the answer was already there in his mind; he hadn't finished with the stones yet. Their strangeness drew him. Up there on the hill were simple choices: do I go right or left? There was no right or wrong, no missed opportunities when walking in a circle.

The same feeling of presence and intention was there even in the solid light of the day. He turned left without thinking why and just walked slipping slightly on the grass, catching himself against the stone, walking on.

The rhythm of his pace drowning out all the chattering in his head. There was just the walking and – to some he supposed it would appear – aimless circling of a small hill scattered with stones on a damp autumn day.

He didn't even have the luxury of being alone. The boy on the red bike had returned and was throwing himself crazily down into the ditch and up again, pivoting on one wheel and yelling all the time to his mum to come and see how magnificent he was; how daring and skilful!

The noise broke into his trance like an awl punched through soft material; the eye of his mind opened again to question himself, his motives for being here, his very life. It was too much … the anger at himself and all he'd carelessly given up exploded in and out again in excessive resentment of this intrusion. He turned sharply, ready to shout at the boy, at his mother for being careless … and looked straight into her lovely eyes.

Flags in the Wind

There are flags waving in the wind, bright banners against the sky over the stupa. The cold catches in the throat like fire; burns into the lungs of the unprepared. Ruby and saffron figures move purposefully up steep wooden steps, clogs chattering, minds still.

We are together and alone in this harsh landscape of the world; barren, yet full of hidden sounds, ghosts of long-past, deeply-remembered lamas. The air inside the temple rich with incense and the sweet smell of the butter-lamps smoking in the corners.

I am full of memories; they spill out across the conscious mind, seep through the barriers of time, rush into the present with their sights and smells; their sounds and the touch of otherness.

We were young, only just aware of what we were doing, bursting with zeal. We raised our voices firmly in the chants, mingling with the older ones, the wiser ones, who paced themselves and understood. Our young tones rising eagerly as the deeper notes carved into the layers of illusion and sought the silence beneath all. Our lama simply smiled knowing we would grow. We bowed our dark heads over the books, under the watching statues of the Bodhisattvas in their niches, and felt the age of everything.

Set free in the afternoons, we circled the mountain like the eagles, walking to release the energy; letting our eyes wander where our feet would never go, up to the highest peaks gold in the sunlight; down into the valleys filled with shade upon shadow of indigo and the pull of worldly life.

When the snows came, we huddled in the long houses and the temple rooms, listening to the force of the storm howling like those other shades in the Bardo. Sometimes even the long horns were not loud enough to rise above the fierce clamour of the moving air battering the mountain; thrusting its fingers, yowling, into our refuge; piercing our prayers with entreaty of its own.

And then would come the crystalline sharpness of the morning when the blizzard had passed, and we were let go out into its brightness, where the blue of the sky arched over the temple behind the flapping flags, and the intensity of the light after the smoke-filled gloom was a benediction.

On one such day he was to come. It was not a day after storm, but in retrospect it felt like it, as if a cloud had been lifted and a sudden silence bestowed upon the earth.

We had been told of his coming the night before in puja by our lama. In our best robes we were to welcome him to our home; our temple. Such excitement among us rarely seen and barely contained. In the morning light we stood on the balconies which hang over the path, crowding the wooden rails, worn smooth by countless hands. Pressed against the edge for the first view of the visitor who had come all this way through the storms of the mountains up to our refuge; to meet our lama. Did we realise then the significance? Only in the sense of prescience which abided in the air; the way in which the old monks moved with surer step.

And then he was there, walking bareheaded up the steep path with the monks who had gone to meet and guide him. We hung over the railing, red-robed elbows touching, and saw the nimbus of his golden hair and heard his laughing voice. As he passed underneath towards the entrance steps he looked up, and, it seemed, straight into my eyes, and what passed then between us was as natural as breathing in the lovely mountain air, and as profound as deep stillness. He was, as suddenly, past and gone into the sanctuary where the lama waited on his dais, and where we went presently to join him in prayer.

The memories tumble away, and once again the noise of the banners snapping in the breeze brings to the waking mind this present moment in another life. Times coalesce and again I follow the monks up the wooden steps into the temple, carrying my camera.

The Idea

The soft rain dripping from rowan berries and the fingers of larch seeps quickly into the mossy ground; gathers momentum in hidden rivulets deep within and reappears between two lichen-covered rocks on the heathered hill. Orange and purple sing with the slick wetness. The stream gathers momentum in the humming air. Somewhere a curlew lifts its arched cry in counterpoint and two black ravens fall in the misty grey towards the loch.

All this viewed in a moment, creates a rich picture, which both changes and remains; an after impression behind the eyes, upon the soul. I can see it now, the slippery roots and sodden earth making the path treacherous; the mountains appearing and disappearing through the haze of hanging cloud.

The most potent shrines are those created where no one else will see them and nothing marks them, except in memory. My icons are the patterns on the stone, my incense the smell of wet bracken and juniper; my chants belong to the emerging spring, the falling rain, the wild birds.

Memory adds the moment of the idea's birth; embellishing it, no doubt, with a ray of light cleaving the heavy sky!

In my mind, having reached the earth, the idea takes off like a startled hare, bounding across the landscape, picking up other creatures in its wake, releasing so much energy!

That I could contain this idea did not occur to me at that moment. It was a creature released and free. Possibly it could never be held? Yet that is exactly what I would do ...

It took a long time to find this spot. Whilst the 'hare' bounded around in springtime abandonment, the 'tortoise' slowly visited different locations, chewed over the possibilities presented, assessed the viability. But finally, both found their way here and came together – with effort and not a little finance – fixed, earthed.

I stretched and stood, looking out over the loch surrounded by hills. The peace enfolding the senses just as the shingle beach enfolded the water. I came back to the present, pleased that soon the children would be here again, for the third year, revelling in the freedom, released into the embrace of the elements.

Picking my way back over the pebbles around the crescent of the bay, stepping over the rushing header streams thick with melt water, and around the mossy boulders, presently the boathouse came into view. The boats would need checking again, and kitting out before tomorrow's influx. From the bay the way led up the slight incline of the wide smooth path to the house, set in a hollow, surrounded by trees and further paths through rhododendron thickets and past stands of juniper and sage. Yes, I had chosen well, all the senses were stimulated by colour and scent and sound; small brooks babbled into the stream and of course the birds called incessantly: the sandpipers, the curlew and the ubiquitous gulls screaming out over the loch.

Into a bright new day the minivans trundled down the steep road through the hills towards the house, brakes screeching. And here they were. First out was Jamie. He was the lively one, I remembered, full of laughter and unthinking joy. Taking in everything in one huge gulp and releasing it in an explosion of sound! Next came Isobel. She rarely made a noise and was as still as a child could be, only when she was out on the water, and especially when she took the tiller and mainsail at the same time, did her smile seem to fill not only her face but her whole body with a light which went beyond joy, approaching something almost transcendent. There were only three this time and last to leave the van was Peter; studious, questioning Peter, always wanting to know, 'Why did we call it 'tacking'?' 'What made the morning mist hang just over the water like that; like a blanket?' He would make his way in the world through understanding it thoroughly, if he got the chance.

Of all the house I was pleased most with their ground floor rooms. Not only did the large windows give views out over the majesty of the mountains and the loch, but I had insisted with the architect that they come right down to the floor, so that the children could, in a few minutes, be out in the pure, scented air of a Scottish morning. Needless to say, 'It was not wise', was the mumbled cry of the builders, but I had the glass strengthened to withstand the winter storms and took the risk. Now, to see the effects made it worthwhile beyond words.

The mild weather continued into the next day, welcoming these children home, hugging them with its warmth and the radiance of light which clear winds and wild places bring. Charlie McDougal, Julia and Sam Bennett had anticipated as usual, 'Och, they know the weather before the weather knows itself', Marie who came to cook proudly told me. So here they were, already down in the boat house when the children arrived; the tall wide doors flung open top and bottom to the path and to the water, and the boats rigged and ready. Jamie and Peter were vying to be first in, Isobel, as usual, content to wait.

I watched as the ceiling hoists were lowered down, and each child winched up in turn out of the heavy wheelchairs and down slowly into the boats. Not quick enough for Jamie of course, whose cries of, 'Faster, faster' were in agreement with the gulls, who also anticipated a good day on the water following the sails! And then they were out, each with their own 'buddy', skimming across the water into the morning. Wave upon wave of unrestricted energy echoing off the hillsides, light streaming behind them in the wake of their freedom.

The Lapis Scarab

The lapis scarab lay on her palm. Her hand lay open in the sharp sunlight slanting across the surface of the café table where she sat. She saw at once a fixed snapshot of the scene: the incessant hooting of car horns, the passing by of bodies, the rise and fall of voices, all a counterpoint to this one still moment.

She remembered the first time she had seen the pure blue of the scarab. She had been painting in the desert. The tour company promised spectacular scenes and did not disappoint: ochres and crimson, burnt orange and magenta, with deep violet brown shadows. She had used huge amounts of these paints and was concerned no one at home would believe the vividness was real. How to capture the great bowl of the sky, or the endless emptiness filled with sand and rock and heat? These were the only thoughts in her mind, which, as the days had passed, had emptied and emptied until only the action of hand and eye remained.

One late afternoon she had walked away from the camp; from the heat of the fire and the men noisily putting together the meal; climbed gradually, the nearest ridge out of the oasis, to a place where she knew she could sit silently and look out across the dunes towards the setting sun. As always, the landscape stretched out all around her, the light intensifying the colours, until she felt she sat at the centre of a cauldron of flame.

It was just as the sun dipped quickly beneath the farthest dune that she saw the horse. It hobbled into the valley below her, obviously very lame and led by a man who looked, even at this distance, to be near exhaustion. As darkness swooped across the desert land, rider and horse slowly rounded the bluff towards the oasis and out of sight. She hastened back herself now, sliding down the slopes as the stars spread out above her in the enormity of heaven.

The camp was filled with fretful activity and noise. She was aware of the men arguing; the horse rearing and bucking in the hands of one of them, and its rider slumped in the sand by the fire. No one, it seemed, could handle the poor thing in its pain. Without thinking she entered the firelight, walking calmly towards it. The men shouted at her, but her eyes were on the stallion and she ignored them. The creature was afraid with the pain, trying not to put his left front leg to the ground, whilst resisting being held by a stranger. She caught his wild eyes and held them, all the while speaking softly in her mind and then, as she drew nearer, gently voicing coaxing words. She moved slowly, but with surety, until she was a yard away and then stopped. The horse became still. 'Let go,' she said to the man holding him. There must have been an unusual authority in her tone because he stepped back into the shadows joining the rest of the now silent watchers. She held her hands out slightly, palms open to the stallion's nose and mouth. He whiffled and she moved to touch him. His coat was matted and standing up, riddled with sweat. Shivers ran along his back. She smoothed his face, his neck and down his leg gently until she came to the nasty gash. The stallion was hers now. He hung his head and was calm under her experienced hands, only the shivers betrayed his pain and exhaustion.

The men had watched carefully with their usual looks of indifference towards women, but they understood her needs and had brought warm water and fresh strips of cloth. They also had the tools she needed and gently she got to work on the wound.

When all was done her arms felt leaden and all her energy spent. The men stepped up then and, now docile, the stallion was let through the darkness to the fences where the other animals were tethered, stamping and shifting in their upright sleep. She knew he would be rubbed down, fed and watered; horses are precious in the desert. When finally she remembered the rider she found him curled up in a blanket by the fire in complete collapse, one arm flung out over the horse's saddle as if protecting a lover.

In the morning, when the excited questions of her fellow artists had all been answered, she found the rider had gone. The stallion, however, was still in the camp and snorted quietly, almost she could believe in welcome, as she came to check on him. The men had accepted her right. Usually proprietorial when it came to the animals, they let her approach; and this was the way of it for the next few days. Each morning she would check the horse before anything else. When her companions went off with the guide for a two-day trek into the foothills, she stayed at the camp; knowing how easily a wound can become infected; not wishing to leave him in the hands of anyone else. In so far as the men could, she earned their respect for this, and gradually the stallion's leg improved. She also gained, bit by bit, the story of his rider. Apparently he had left at day break the morning after he had stumbled into the camp, borrowing another horse and racing the sun towards the next oasis in the foothills, where his mother was dying. When she heard this from the young boys who tended the smelly camels, she understood; only such a thing could have separated him from this proud creature whose leg she tended each day and whose name, she discovered, was 'Desert Flame'.

The evening before she was to return to Cairo with the party, she came back from the same dunes as before to find the horse gone. His rider had returned, saddled up the 'Flame', whose leg was now almost fully healed, and gone again, back wherever he had come from, leaving a small blue scarab lying on her pillow with a note.

Now, six months later, she was back from England; the desert drawing her like a moth to fire. The lapis scarab felt hot in her hand as it lay in the sun and she shifted. A dark hand came down covering her palm and a voice said quietly:

'Flame will be pleased to see his rider's wife.'

Wolf-run

The wolves were closing in. He ran with his heart clamouring to escape, through the dark woods, between and over branches, fear lifting his feet over all obstacles without any control ... his mind too full of what pursued him. His feet did not betray him, but the wind did, skittering around, whispering above him, carrying his scent back. He ran on ... to the sound the trees made chaffing together and whipping around in the breeze ... the wolves were silent. And then another sound found its way to him ... water ... the river was close, the noise of water rushing over rocks lent him just a little more strength and speed.

He reached the bank and plunged straight in without breaking his stride, throwing himself into the river's swirling flow as he threw a prayer of thanks upwards for its deliverance, swimming out into the current towards the further shore with flailing powerful strokes. His prayer continued to be answered when, after some flailing moments, he found a submerged trunk to catch; to pull him up onto the opposite bank.

He followed the river down towards its mouth, towards the sea, hoping there to find a boat, a raft even, that would take him further towards his goal. The wolves left far behind. Their cubs would go hungry tonight.

Later, stumbling in the darkness of the forest he heard the welcome roar of waves against the shore; smelled the sea-wrack and the sharp salt wind. As the trees began to lean inwards, following the prevailing gales, he hesitated. The king would not thank him for rushing headlong into the arms of his enemies, no matter how urgent the message was. Better to stop here in the dark and wait for the dawn, or the light of the moon; there were other wolves out on the hunt tonight!

He moved into the blackest shadows and sat, facing the sea, breathing steadily and quietly, calming his heart. Nothing stirred except the wind. The night drew down and inwards around him, stalking his resolution, baiting his fear. But his breath grew still, centred. He became the tree, the ground, the wind. The old training from the priest, long ago in another land, came back without effort, and another prayer escaped heavenwards from his lips: silent thanks to that wrinkled lama who sat patiently for so long, helping him gain control. Never had it been more needed than now, with all the King's enemies close.

The moon rose slowly, glimpsed between the branches, scattered light, gold, then white, across the water, as the waves rolled in. Now he crept to the edge, where the beach shelved down, watched each wave catch the light and roll it to the shore like silk across the skin of the sand. No footsteps marred the smoothness of that sand, and just where the rocks at the curve of the bay reached their bony fingers out into the water, he saw the boat. A small skiff, tied loosely, rising and falling with the sea. Now was the moment. He left the safety of the trees and moved parallel with them until the boat lay before him and then, with all the calm he could find, he moved down low, at a run, across the strand towards it. Still no one; still no sound above the rushing pull and hiss of the water. Quickly now he loosed the rope and was over the side and in, reaching for the oars and pulling away into the heavy swell, every sinew stretched with effort.

Just as he thought himself safe, just as the headland was almost rounded, he heard above the slap of waves, the cries of hounds and men. They were near the beach, coming fast through the forest. Would the tide take him round the point. No time to think. He pulled the oars in; lay down in the boat, and let everything go. Let them think the boat was abandoned and had slipped its moorings in the gales. Let the tide carry him out, not in again ... He dare not look. But he could feel the swell. He could also hear the pounding against the rocky cliffs, and he knew in that moment that wolves' teeth may take many forms.

The teeth bit down upon the boat with a savagery which knocked him senseless for a brief span and sent him plunging into the grip of the sea. He fought it; wrestled with the waves as they sucked at his bone and blood; forced his tired arms to pull him down, away from the rocks, away from sight of the shore. His breath held tightly like a lover, released slowly, reluctantly, until at the last moment there was peace; a drifting upwards towards the blue-green light, to float on the still waters of a hidden bay beyond the wolves' hunger.

When darkness came again, he was sheltered in a cave half way up the steep cliffs which stretched along all this shoreline. He had clambered all day over sea-wrack and boulders slick with the aftermath of the tide, slipping and sliding, grazing his hands and once his face, yet buoyant with hope. The wolves did not devour him – neither nature nor man – and now there was a chance. Eventually, as it grew dark with cloud and approaching night, he had looked for a place to climb and found this cave in which to rest.

Sometime in the half-sleep darkness he fancied he heard the wolves again, but it was only the sea wind howling through the blowholes on the shore. The wind had scoured the sky clear; stars speckled the night and the moon's light reached into the cave, touching the rock walls and firing the crystals embedded there, so that he fell asleep again in muted rainbow light.

He left the shelter at first light, clambering up the last part of the cliff, the sea opalescent with mist below him. Gaining the earthy overhang at the top he paused, listening ... to the sea swell far below ... to the gulls' lament. To his right he could see how the next headland held the end of the long bay, his destination. Not far now. He calculated quickly: one day through the forest; one day over the rocky shore beneath the cliffs and now today ... yes ... one last run and he would be in time. He began to run again ... pounding the soft turf of the cliff-top; breathing easily, the salt wind dispersing the fog of tiredness from his mind as the sea mist dissolved with the rising sun.

At the crest of the headland, he found the sea spread out before him and there it was ... almost unbelievably after all that had happened ... a small dot against the grey, but surely it was her … the boat coming quietly, purposefully into the arms of the bay, bringing the bride to her king.

He took the short, steep route down towards the waiting shore, his mind running over the words he was to relay; the directions he was to give: how the king, fighting this heavy war, was sorry not to meet her himself, but that he had sent his most trusted knight to accompany her on the journey until he could be with her.

Suddenly, as he rounded a heather-clad rock near the shore, his senses were disturbed by a prickling in the air; a slight shift of sound from behind. He dropped instantly into the rough cover at the foot of the boulder and saw them – the men and the powerful dogs – pouring over the top, on the hunt still, for him. He glanced seaward. She had not yet come into their sight, nor would she! In one fierce moment, almost of joy, he ran out from cover; leapt away from the sea, inland, noisily crashing through bracken and fern, arms flailing, hearing the wolves cry out with their greed at finding him and rush downwards to give chase. He would do this one last thing for her, for his king. God give him the strength so that until the sea was far behind and she was safe, he would make the wolves run for their kill!

The Wedding

The whispered conversation beneath the open window drifted up on the wind, along with the overpowering scent of lilies ... Sophie couldn't help but hear ... her senses overwhelmed by the fragrance and the implication of the exchange ... the wedding ...

How could this have happened? She leaned closer on the window sill, and caught one further word ... September. So that was it then ... a date had been set.

The long, carpeted hallway stretched blankly ahead of her, flowers adorning the tables in tightly packed displays, clashing colours, mingling with the long-dead smell of ancestry and tradition. Her head swam, the odour from the window threatened to overwhelm her. She turned and ran, blindly, with years of practise, down the length of the room, through the double doors, and into the dark, mothy regions of the library, where there were no flowers, only the smell of leather and beeswax; of oil on the wooden floor, and dust on the top shelves where Betsy, the maid, refused to reach. She sank into one of the huge chairs, her head pounding, and the light prickling behind her closed eyes, like motes of dust. Sophie breathed deeply and more deeply, willing her head to stop its movement, and her mind to stop remembering the words: wedding ... September ... how could she bear it!

Sometime later, when the dusk had drawn in, and the bats flitted outside the long, mullioned windows, she came to herself more, though she did not really know what that meant any longer. The room was cold, and shivering, she pulled her cramped body up and stumbled towards the table on which the old Bible sat, squarely authoritarian and forbidding. Not really knowing why she did it, Sophie opened the book at random, and, in the remaining light from the casement read the words: 'The kingdom of heaven is like unto a certain king, which made a marriage for his son. And sent forth his servants to call them that were bidden to the wedding ...'. the synchronicity of this felt to Sophie like a conspiracy; she even searched the page and the table to see if someone had marked this place to be found, before she realised her foolishness and a kind of dread took over.

The light broke sharply and painfully the following morning – the sun seeming to rise tropically straight up into a cloudless, searing sky – revealing Sophie's sprawled form on the library couch:

'Come on Miss ... wake up now ...', Betsy spoke loudly, breaking into Sophie's blurred mind.

'The master's back and he wants to see you straight away.' The urgency in Betsy's tone reached through the veil of forgetfulness. Sophie tried, but could not escape the memories which thrust forward the moment she opened her eyes. Betsy's concern only adding to the feeling of inevitability.

In the morning room the long windows were flung wide already and the sun cast bars of light and shade across the wooden floor. Sophie walked down one of these shadowy lines towards the seated figure outlined against the light. Her guardian did not turn, or look up, but motioned curtly to the opposite seat and began to speak in a voice where no accent, no rise and fall, no passion lay, just words devoid of life:

'It has been decided that your wedding to your cousin will take place in September in the church on the estate. Aunt Heloise will help you prepare. She has sufficient funds for your needs.'

A pause … whilst the sound of bees in the honeysuckle filled the room:

'That will be all.'

Dismissed, like a servant, Sophie rose and left as she had arrived, in shadow, straightway, her shoes echoing in counterpoint to the bees' drone. She walked, as in a dream, through the hall and out of the door into the morning. Without seeing, trying not to feel, she kept on walking between the box hedges and under the yew trees; down the long path towards the sound of the sea against the crags, and the cliffs which ended the pasture in abrupt, feet-tingling heights.

Sometime later – time seeming somehow to have become disjointed, fragmented, peculiar – Sophie found herself watching the rise and fall of gannets and guillemots, fulmars and gulls as they floated out over the ocean. There was something very odd with a world where a girl – trapped and bound – could see and sense such enormous freedom. Yet were the birds truly free. Free to fly, yes, but bound nonetheless by their needs and all the responses passed down to them by parent birds, from the egg to their first flight. Not much difference then ... how could freedom be found in being thus controlled?

Sophie set her mind free. In her thoughts she shook off the sense of outside control. Watching the birds glorying in their flight she began to understand what being captured really was ... it was when you allowed circumstances to dictate your thoughts and feelings so that the moment lost its magic. Suddenly the birds were there, truly there in her sight. Movement, joy, freedom ... they took the moment as they took the wind, and used it, made it their own, took from it what they could and let it go. And she could do the same! Nothing which was 'planned' for her could take away her inner freedom to extract from each blessed moment her own response.

From her pocket she took the missive which she carried with her always and opened it ... at random ... to the miracle of the loaves and fishes and the calming of the storm.

Voices

There are voices all around us, following their own paths amongst the heather, rock and birch. They are distant, but there, like the first sight of the sea at the edge of the moors, appearing and disappearing with the dips and curves of the road.

We sit in a glade, with the white trunks as sentinels and pillars, twisted in and out with low clumps of blueberry and more solid grey-green rocks, half-buried in the bright moss. And the voices come and go, first this side, where the land falls into the old quarry, and then on the other where the white sky appears behind the trees on the horizon. We sit in another world, unseen and unseeing, witnesses to the sounds of men. Are we their ghosts, or are their whispers only shadows of the mind's remembering?

'We first came to this place when we were young', she said. Then, following my own thoughts: 'I half believe the voices are us as we were then, laughing, playing, innocent …'.

Her voice trails off, slipping into the poignant silence of remembering … I wait, whilst the quiet moments extend, filtering out like the sunlight, between the trees towards the distant sea.

She is still so young, and I am like the quarry, worked out, full of heavy, unwanted remains. It is easy for her to reminisce; her thoughts also have a future. But me, I am impatient, there is too little time left. I move roughly, suddenly, so she lifts her head, and I see her eyes return from those childhood days; see her focus on my face and turn away embarrassed.

We are so close, and yet we might as well be as separate as the hidden voices all around us. Whatever made me think we could meet? And here in this place of phantoms and children's fancies? I stand to leave, but do not remember where the path is. It seems the trees are guardians of more than dreams; they present a united shield against the ordinary world, and in that moment of confusion she makes a bridge; holds out her hand.

'Dad?' she entreats softly, and all the years go rolling back to one hot summer day and a tousle-headed tomboy of a child, fallen in a ditch and asking for a hand up.

'Do you remember ...', we both speak at once and need say no more ...

Unexpected Radiance

The sea rippled with the ancient light of the years, lifting itself into the arms of the sun; mesmeric, shifting patterns coalesced and dissolved with the wind's caress.

Nothing could have prepared him for how he felt. Patterns shifted across the pebbles; his mind rearranged impressions from the past hours.

The rock glinted as waves slid across its face, phantom lights. The cave had been like that, full of unexpected radiance. The trek to it, in the early morning, was by contrast hot and full of dust. The cave, high up in the mountains, was half-hidden amongst the scrub and wiry bushes; boulders tumbling down either side of the rocky steps up from the harsh golden ground, where grasses grew in early spring. Occasionally he heard a goat bleating and the ever-present rattle of the cicadas coruscated the air as the sun rose higher.

The jagged entrance to the cave itself gave him the impression of a cut in the fabric of the land but, even then not a desecration, rather a ritual mark for those who could understand.

The radiance in the cave came from the crystals embedded in the rock. That much he knew as he squeezed carefully round the broken boulders at the entrance and was surprised by the light inside. There were one or two narrow funnelled openings upwards to the hot mountain air, and down these shafts light sufficient to awake the fires in the stones and set the mica glinting. Wondrous indeed, but not unreal. The crystals could be named, could be analysed and their properties understood. The precise way in which the sunlight refracted in them was known to science. But this was just the beginning ... in preparation the lights had been lit.

He watched the movement of the sea and remembered how compelling the reflections had been; how he had sat on the cold rock floor and become absorbed in them for a long time. From time to time, even inside the cave and as involved as he was, he would still register the sound of the cicadas, but gradually another noise penetrated, of hooves clattering against rock and the small scattering reverberation of pebbles loosed into the valley below. Many goats roamed these mountains, even nowadays when shepherding was less common throughout Greece, so it wasn't until the air changed subtly at the entrance of the cave that he turned to see what was there.

And this is where his mind now faltered ... skitted away from remembering ... tried to focus on the solidity of what is known; what is actually here ... but he was now staring at the fluctuating sea, where nothing was still, nothing was the same from one moment to the next, and he had seen what he had seen ... standing at the cave mouth not a goat or sheep, though the hooves were there of course, but a Pan-like figure, regarding him with a calm gaze as old as the earth itself, touching his mind with query. His mind came alight with recognition of legends almost forgotten; those stories still kept alive in these wild places by the people who knew the land, who did not succumb to the banality and cynicism of the electronic world, but walked where the old ones once strode fearlessly along the same paths, under the same sun.

All this passed through his mind in a moment as the figure stood still before him and the light danced in his mind, and then it was all gone. The sun must have dipped below the peaks; the crystals lost their glow; he/it was gone. By the time he had recovered his wits enough to scramble to the entrance there was nothing to be seen. His eyes adjusted quickly to the daylight, but there was nothing on the path. Nothing moving on the mountainside below. He suddenly felt enervated, drained of all feeling and thought, as the crystals were emptied of their light. The journey back down the mountain seemed impossible to take, like plunging into fog after being in the sun. He looked out beyond the silvery hills, where he could just see the blue/ green ocean and longed for its cool waters.

Now he was here, beside the sea. The harsh mountain behind him. The wind beginning to ease and the flat turquoise calm spreading out to the horizon ... one more memory waiting to float in onto the sand of the present ... as he had lurched almost unseeingly down the narrow path, from somewhere far above he had heard rippling down on the heavy-laden air, the sound of pipes.

Michaelmas Daisies

Michaelmas daises like a hazy spring dawn sky, dappled pink here and there by the light, stretched beyond her sight either side of the long path. The walls, still warm from the late September sun, were profuse with rose hips, succulent, carmine, tempting. She stopped, haunted by the soft as well as the bright colours; one season blending into another without the intervening harsh notes of winter.

There was green still, but not for long. Soon the brown and grey would come; the sky would darken; the light would drain from the land and her skin would lose the soft blush of summer; would become pallid, her heart's vitality dwindled. Fitting then, as she stood in this sombre mood, that the garden mirrored her own anticipated time of separation and cold, when trees would stand isolated from each other, all the abundance of meadow and leafy bush gone from between them and their stark trunks left to face the storms alone.

The daisies shifted in the wind and revealed their yellowing leaves. The rose stems were almost bare. Alongside the paths, the rills ran quietly in their shallow beds, already carrying leaves.

She turned away to look out across the gardens to the pastures beyond and the hills rising towards the west, where the sun dipped fingers of cloud in gold and red and painted the skyline with the colours of a summer gone. Overhead a bright skein of geese arrowed south, their cries echoing in the valley; the sound, both mournful and at the same time hauntingly beautiful. The twilight lingered on the tops of the distant trees, in the fragile air still vibrating with the cries of the geese and the harsher sounds of the rooks coming back quarrelling to their beech trees for the night.

Somewhere beyond the hedges a car's engine revved briefly, breaking the mood. She turned … and suddenly he was there before her, this man she had come to love, who she was soon to lose. He stepped out of the darkness of her thoughts into the light from the stars already pricking their way across the sky. She couldn't see him clearly, but she knew him well: the casual air betraying strength, the calm smile lifting the corners of his eyes in gentle mockery of himself and life in general.

He stood unsmiling now, uncertain of his welcome, beyond her reach … after all, the argument about his going had been fierce and damaging. But this was not his home. There was no work for a fisherman here in the Yorkshire Dales and he was cold. And now, seeing him shadowy against the amethyst flowers gradually fading in the gloom, her muscles ached with the memory of the many lovely nights spent dancing beneath these same stars in the Mediterranean warmth and ached also with the effort to hold herself from him now.

Nothing more could be said or done. The silence, the stillness was between them like a halted universe; a stopped clock; a fixed season where nothing but the moment existed, nothing changed or moved ... except already he was receding; the night deepening, the mists springing up from the water and spreading across the path between them, and with the mist the quiet, ghostly flight of a hunting owl. She blinked and awoke.

The shutters were open and dazzling sunlight streamed across the loose sheet. Disorientated, she turned her head to the side following the shaft of light to where it hit the wall by the side of the bed and there lit up a brightly gilded icon in a small niche. She reached for it and saw carved into the wood the inscription Agios Michaelos. In the vivid colours of the sun the angel saint stood proudly with the dragon lying at his feet.

Turning the other way, she looked into his brown eyes, sad with the question which lay unanswered between them. In her mind the daisies still glowed faintly in the dusk and the trees lifted solitary trunks towards the lonely indifferent stars ... dragons take many forms she thought, remembering her fears ...

'England will be cold', she murmured with a smile. As his eyes gleamed with a hope suddenly rekindled, 'Yes', she said.

Leap of Faith

The red-legged chough soared, palmate against the widening blue, twisted, and dropped down, down ... over the cliff and was gone. All around the sweet smell of heather and sheep-clipped gorse filled the air with memory, whilst the sea boomed below, flinging upwards the occasional spume ... and seabird!

And as the bird, the recollection flipped up, turning over and over in the forefront of her mind ...

It had been a day like no other, when all the elements which make life good had come together in one place. The warmth of the sun, the purpled hills reaching down to the sea, air redolent with scent and so pure it almost hurt to breathe ...

When the dog appeared, bounding over the hill, the infectious spirit of the creature externalised her joy, but when the dog didn't slow down as it came rushing towards the cliff edge, she was galvanised into flinging herself in its path, grabbing at the fur and holding on as the dog skidded its front paws over the grassy rim of the rocks. It wriggled; she held on ... 'So, you think you're a bird do you old thing!' she panted, and was rewarded with a face lick.

'Thank God!' the man's voice reached her from some way off, as he raced obviously in pursuit of the would-be 'bird', who finally managed to escape and race towards him in excitement at being found. Julia collapsed in the grass and laughed, and eventually man with dog now firmly on the lead, joined her.

To sit then, in companionable silence, with a stranger on the top of a cliff in the wilderness of Jura, was unusual to say the least. For Julia it was unthinkable. A broken engagement; a failed marriage and nowadays a love of solitude, gave her the kind of outer shell which made people back off, but the dog, it seemed, had broken through with his death-wish run ... bringing his master along for the ride.

And that was where it had begun of course. A discovered mutual love of all things wild, of the stillness at the heart of life and the comedy which often transforms meaninglessness into pleasure, meant that Julia's shell stayed open and David (and the dog) became part of the pearl inside. From that first scent-laden moment, life glistened iridescently and love streamed out to encompass everyone they met. The only problem was distance.

David had sailed to the island by boat. Mooring in one of the sea lochs and skinny-dipping in its icy waters. Julia had come by car and was staying at the hotel. Once their holidays were over David sailed back to Oban and Julia took the plane to Jersey. It was far from ideal, but their jobs dictated separation, and neither wanted to move.

As often as time allowed they commuted back and forth, squeezing a week here and there, and sometimes feigning sickness in order to prolong their time together. But it was inevitably wearing. It produced short tempers and tears, where joy should have been, and it came to an end in a startling fashion.

One day David was gone. He didn't answer his phone. Calls to his parents in Inverness produced no answers. Even a desperate visit to Oban one bleak March day, with the winds whipping down off the mountains, revealed nothing; the house was shut. Worse, with some trepidation, Julia had approached David's dour employer only to find David had resigned. There was nothing to do except to go back to Jersey and forget.

But forgetting is not so easy when you love. You can kid yourself with distracting activity; you can try to mask your true feelings with anger or self-recrimination, but the heart open is like the helter-skelter run of an excitable dog … no matter the cliff, the steep drop, the lack of wings … it seeks to fly. It may be bruised. It may die, but it has to leap.

So although her mind argued otherwise, now in May Julia had come back to Scotland and explored again all the places where they had been happy. She had even gone down to the loch where David's boat had been moored, expecting to see the furled sails and the still water shadows of the hull rippling in the breeze, tugging at anchor. But the water lay empty like an open beseeching palm between the hills.

Now as she sat on the cliff top with the horse tethered behind her, she found the scene strangely comforting, as if something of David remained on this cliff where it all began. There was a pull ... an echoing chord, not just from the scent of heather, but in the wind; in the way the sunlight caught at the sea and tossed it sparkling against the rocks.

After a while, when the horse came nuzzling at her back, she remounted and trotted further along the rough edge, round the knoll at the point and up into the line of hills beyond, following the rough paths carefully until she came to where the land opened out on the far side of the island. Drawing the horse to a standstill, she sat looking across the hinterland to the distant line of sun-bright sea. The light here was going, but the sun still flowed in patterns across the moorland, etched the rocks below the ridge, caught the tops of the few trees by the remote shore, and far, far away outlined one white sail. The horse took a step and she reined it back, their shadows flowing down the slope. When she looked again the white sail was gone.

The Swing of the Lantern

There were ways in which the swinging of the lantern reminded him of the prison. There longed-for water arrived with the jailor's ambling stride in the gloom of the tunnel. Back and forth the precious liquid swung in the can, slopping, toying with his fears ... not good to think so ... a distraction which could turn into danger ... he clamped down firmly on the memory ... control ... keep the darkness at bay.

The lantern light revealed the bowls of great trees beside the path. Occasionally it flashed back from rocky outcrops; mica glinting faintly and then gone, back into the unnatural dark. Eyes glinted, watching his progress with the veiled intensity of the hunted, or the hunter. He hurried on, pressing thought into the recesses of his mind; focused on the ground, the placing of his feet; on the lantern's coruscating light, not the recurring shadows.

More rocks now, his steps echoing between them, their bulk looming higher and closer overhead. He should have felt safer, but the canyon was deep, long and cold, filled with slippery, dank earth, which sucked at his boots. An involuntary gasp escaped as he caught an elbow on projecting stone, the sound rebounding, distorting away into the hidden distance. The lantern swung wildly in his hand, and went out ... Instantly the prison door of his mind swung open and shut with incredible speed, trapping him in his own personal hell, such that not for some eternal, heart-clamouring moments would it register that which his eyes could see: a distant glow, a blessed, blessed light! The 'cell door' opened; awareness flooded in … he was there. The whisper of a breeze reached out from the distant source of light, gently touched his face and dried the wetness there. Ahead would be meadows and sunshine and freedom …

The Spotlight

Sam strode down towards the forest, and, silent as a wraith – his footfalls muffled by the spongy needles which layered the path – he entered the trees.

The sounds of the moorland diminished behind him, until there was nothing but the occasional flap of wings high up in the branches above, or the sudden sharp breaking of a desiccated twig. The air was still, warm, fragrant with resin.

As the forest deepened, gloom settled all around him; no light from any direction, except above. Only now and then, between the trees' straight trunks, a golden pool lit the forest floor, where sunlight reached down. Sam couldn't but think, 'Like spotlights', though the memory of that time was painful and once triggered it had to run its weary course … he hadn't worked since it happened; couldn't bear to since Andy died … a fellow thespian, they had shared the stage.

Despite himself, Andy was drawn to one of these islands of light. Like an addict's lure, it beckoned him to be there again where the dust motes dance in the beams and the spiders' webs glisten. He stood in the warmth of the sun, with the dark auditorium of trees all around, silently waiting and the words came unbidden to his mind: 'Out, out brief candle, life's but a walking shadow, a poor player, that struts and frets his hour upon the stage and then is heard no more …' Andy would be heard no more; the stage lighting support falling, cutting off his bright light, his hour upon the stage ended, and with it, Sam's also. Caught in the dusty circle of light Sam stretched his voice to reach to the furthest darkness and cried Andy's name, startling the doves in the branches above, shattering the pent-up silence like a storm breaking in the heavy-laden summer air. And the ghosts awakened, listening to his pain.

Eventually, Sam found himself walking again, following another glimmer of light until the forest thinned and he stepped out onto the moor, to the smell of hot gorse and honey heather; into the brilliance of light. The lizards ran for cover along the dry stones of the wall, and the sound of a buzzard circling against the blue sky echoed across the grasses. He looked up, squinting against the glare, and saw not just one bird, but another, higher still, soaring …

The echo lingered and took shape in Sam's mind and he heard another's voice, an answering cry to his own in that sun-filled glade back in the forest: 'Be you … be you.' With tears flowing freely now, Sam took his phone from his pocket. The email from his agent read: 'Don't be a fool, Sam. They want you for Macbeth! What do I tell them?' He looked back towards the dark forest, and, as the mewing cries of the buzzards receded across the moorland hills, he texted: 'Say yes'.

The Priest and the Boy

The sun glistens on the body of the old priest, bent double over the young one before him; the child and the man silhouetted against the deep turquoise of the sea. Age and youth, freedom and restraint, all seem, at this moment as one. The priest sighs as he pats the boy's head. The boy stares – what is he thinking? – at the black-robed figure, the cowled face, the sun on the brown skin like an aura.

Against the backdrop of the blue sea, the large pots rimmed with light curl their ancient shapes; red-brown against viridian; one fluid and changing; the other fixed and still. The spectrum of life and interchangeable: the sea at this moment and from this distance looking as unmoving as a swathe of rock; the land, the pots, the old man and the young boy shimmering against the blue in the heat of the day.

Over my shoulder a woman speaks quietly, 'This is my only son, Stephanos. And this is the priest of our village, our Papa.' I wait. 'There is nothing I would not do for them both'. Her simple words catch at my breath as the heat does, fierce with love. 'They are precious'. My unspoken acceptance of this fact seems to unlock something and, more surely now, she speaks, her voice echoing off the wall, 'My son is the youngest in our village now. He is our future and the Papa instructs him for it. Oh, it is not so much in words, you understand, but in his ways.'

We watch the two male figures in silence, heads bending together edged with the vivid light. The woman has seated herself on the concrete wall beside me, black against white, as uncomplicated as her words. My sideways look asks for more, and she says softly: 'Georgios is Stephanos father. He and the Papa meet in the kafeneion every Friday and talk and play backgammon.' There is something about this woman's voice which paints pictures, and suddenly I can see them, hear them: the clack of the counters, the rough Greek voices which always sound as if they are arguing, the brilliance of the stars beginning their nightly climb up the sky.

The woman continues to share her life with me, a stranger, 'Georgios tells me the Papa is wise. I only know that he understands my Stephanos and what we need in this village. That is enough and it is good.'

Somewhere a dog barks and a Greek expletive cuts through the air, dislodging the woman, the boy and the priest. All move at once. The woman looks briefly at me and calls to her son to come for his dinner if the Papa has finished with him. The priest rises stiffly, his long white beard catching the light as he turns towards the sea. The boy reaches out to hold him in the way that Greek men do, without embarrassment, with easy grace. 'Avrio', I hear the priest call and the boy's smile is like a mirror image of the sun … easy to love, even for me. There is a complicated knot around my heart, and in that moment one tiny thread is pulled clear.

Later, lying in the stifling heat of the room, with the air conditioning churning without effect and the weight of memory pressing down on my chest, the knot, however, seems just as secure. The mind is clever, but it loses its way where pain is and becomes instead cunning. It returns to the way which will feel the least, trust the least. The image of the boy and the priest, the love of the mother, the eternal stars, all fade into a place where there is no meaning. It is hard to hold on. They slip like phantoms, dissolving into the bleached distance.

Consciousness returns with the fresh air of evening as the light fades. The village awakes, the cicadas' song is muted and the frogs in the rocky clefts of the surrounding hills take over.

There is only one taverna. The centre of life at night time, where young and old and every age in between gather to eat and laugh, and pull apart all the stupid legislations by 'those people who know nothing in Athens', and sigh over the young leaving and the tourists' stupidity. The plane trees whisper overhead and coloured lights swing crazily in their branches.

My table is in a corner by the old black oven where the bread is still baked in the mornings. It is hotter here, but more secluded. The Greeks do not understand. At first they kept trying to include me in their parties, to join them in their dancing, but now they leave me alone and just smile uncomprehendingly and shrug. It is better this way. Sometimes I read, but usually I drink and stare beyond the check-clothed tables and the lights to the sea where the boats of the octopus fishers are faint against the dark and sometimes the phosphorescence leaves trails across the inky water.

Tonight all is the same. There is comfort in this. Two old men sit legs akimbo either side of the kitchen door, with beads sliding continuously through their swollen jointed hands. Sentinels, they guard a portal into a past age. The long ice cream fridge whirrs next to one of them. On the other side a table holds receipts and a card machine. They ignore these, glare at each customer proprietarily and are silent with age and lives hard-lived. I feel like them, but without the comfort of the beads, the promises of prayer. My hands are still. I had today but one short time of resurrection, when something stirred and was quickly gone.

And then I see them, the boy Stephanos gliding up the steep path like a skier, weaving from one side to the other in exuberance, his mother calmly behind, and alongside a tough-looking man, burnished copper by work in the sun, Georgios. They move into the light from the taverna, this family, and I feel I know them. The mother of Stephanos, through her quiet words, has brought me into their lives. She sees me staring and smiles. Without realising, I smile back and then they are there, crowding into my space, introductions, chairs scraping on the flags, retsina ordered. They ignore my hesitation, ignore the signs. As easily as the woman spoke to me earlier in the day, they seat themselves, draw me towards them. 'She is lonely. She is lost', I hear the woman say quietly to the father of Stephanos. 'You and your strays!', he replies with laughter in his voice. They do not think I understand, but all at once I do. Here is kindness. Here is love. Under my tee-shirt something seems to unravel.

The sea is spangled with diamonds as the moon rises; the air hums with warmth. And then, from the higher village where the square opens out in front of the church comes a sound I will never forget, is imprinted on my psyche as forever the moment of completeness, the sound of the priest chanting.

'Listen to the Papa', cries Stephanos.

The taverna is quiet, the worry beads are still in the hands of the old men. The sounds of entreaty and praise rise to fill the night.

'Amen' we reply.

The Pilgrimage

In the distance the statuesque shapes of the sycamore trees curl against the bright grass as it slopes up the hill. The scent of larch and pine flows sharply upwards over the ridge. Looking down between his feet, patches of iridescent green moss leap out of the darkness amongst the rocky rooted beds of the forest floor. He hangs there above the trees like a spider caught in a web of sunlight; gossamer strands of memory hold him in place far from the ground, pinned against the rock on a narrow ledge.

This is where it happened then … a little higher and he would see the last things she saw before she fell exactly a year ago today. Nothing much would have changed since then in this wild place, unknown to many climbers. And yet everything had changed for him.

It had taken him a day to clamber his way to this spot – a day of anguish and anticipation mingled with his sweat. So that the cool air on the mountainside was a blessing and he slipped back easily into the rhythm of movement against gravity: reaching a hand above to the next crevice, dimly discerned in the rock face; pulling at the same time as his free leg swung out to the higher foothold; barely stopping before the next move, the next shift of weight upwards. And now there was not much further to go to find the place.

He turned his head into the dark red of the millstone grit; felt the roughness of the rock under his hands, against his cheek, before reaching once more for the deep gash which led the way up eventually towards the top. It was half way up the shallow chimney which the fissure became that it had happened. As he climbed thoughts slipped in and out of his conscious mind, how her parents would not speak to him now, blaming her passion for climbing on him; barely acknowledging him at the cremation. How he had raged at them when they turned him away from their house without one thing of hers to cherish.

Eventually he pulled himself to the small outcrop of rock in the crevice where they said she had lost her footing. Balancing against the face he gazed again at the dark shapes of the trees below and the view of the horizon rolling away towards the high bleak moors. This was her final vision, fragrant with life, yet impersonal. Did she have time to witness the way the trees leaned into the rock, hugging themselves to its contours? Did she have time to think ... of him?

There was only one safe direction to go to negotiate a way to the top of the ridge and after a while he supposed he should take it. Extending his left hand out to its furthest extent to grip the edge of the only crack available he hauled himself back onto the rock face above the cleft and paused. His hand had touched something different in the crack and for a moment adrenalin pumped so fast into his body it froze all movement. Solid rock gave way to something soft at the end of the crack, and what yielded on the rock was dangerous. After several frightening moments, when he knew he would survive this, he was at last able to shift his right foot into a more secure hold, and with his weight firmly to the right, was able to move his left fingers until he held and drew out of the crack a piece of paper wrapped tightly around something else. Stepping carefully, he was able to release himself backwards to the main chimney and the outcrop, where it was safer to stop and peel away the paper he'd found to reveal … a ring! … her ring … the one he'd thought lost from her battered body … the one she had cried over when he placed it on her finger the night they were engaged.

He stared transfixed at the single sparkling gem, undimmed by its year in the dark, his mind in turmoil, whilst the wind carried small sounds around and by him which he never heard. And then two things became suddenly clear … the memory that her autopsy had revealed a virulent inoperable cancer, which no one had known about, and alongside that he realised she must have known he would come; she trusted him, knew he would make this journey to see what she had seen and feel the rock where the last imprint of her warm hand had lain. And with those thoughts, the sudden incontrovertible fact that she had not fallen, but leapt willingly into death after doing what she loved … it was a benediction.

He looked down at the paper in his hand and noticed through a haze of tears that she had written some words on it; words from the soundtrack of the climbing film 'The Wildest Dream', which they had watched together that first night, kissing and crying and laughing equally.

He read them now aloud triumphantly to the wilderness, to the birds soaring on the westerly wind:

'I brought you with me all these miles I've climbed ... on the edge of heaven I will wait for you ... on the edge of heaven find me there.'

As she leapt backwards, did she look up the cliff, as he did now, and see how the wild grasses on the top were stalks of feathered light blown like surf towards a distant inland shore?

The Choice

The translucent, blue-green of the curling wave – a moment's bliss – its beauty one ephemeral sigh along the shore. So longed for, so fleetingly re-born. On the headland, the desert colours of the summer wilderness, a contrast of orange and hot yellow, splashed with the white of rock and boulder, the dusty red of earth. The palette of this landscape far from subtle: lines of deep shadow and brilliant light, apart from the sea's horizon, where the waxen sky melted into a watery haze.

Although she knew the physics, there was still the magic of the turning moment when a wave catches light, refracts, bends, displaces and such a vibrant colour spills into being. Magic was needed in her life right now, as it hung suspended, waiting for signs. Should she take the wave, fold it into her pattern and release that life into her veins, or stay with the golden, stable land, her blood enriched by its strength? An age-old dilemma, as old as the consciousness of the mind.

In her peripheral vision a bird floated out from the land and over the sea; no movement discernible of its wings, just a graceful spiral upwards on the hot air, carrying it further and eventually beyond her sight.

The bird was a new dimension in the landscape, neither rock, nor sea, but a choice which used their boundaries and yet transcended them. The bird knew the physics also; knew the way that heat rises, knew how to use it to move beyond it without effort. The bird did not doubt its awareness, its knowledge, and when it was so high that the updraft was gone, why, it would engage those wings and fly …

To have such unquestioning faith in one's wings! She fancied she could see it now, slipping out over the ocean on a cool wind, the heat of the land left behind and the fish-filled sea rolling far below.

Recess

The path was steep and so deeply cut into the rock and soil that from the side of the cliff it could not be seen; sometimes it narrowed until one foot had to be placed carefully above the other as she climbed. Rounding a smooth boulder, at one point, she placed her hand, almost reverently upon it and felt the thrumming, whether of the sea far below, or the wind, she could not be sure.

There was just one place where the path opened out, where she could step off to the side and rest. Here she leaned into the land; let it take her into itself, so that when the time came to move on, she was calm.

The last few steps however were tough and she hauled herself up over the grassy edge with relief, expecting the wind to intensify, but unusually all was still, as if the climb had been enough of a test for now.

It was another sense which overwhelmed her, as she lay on the short, wind-bitten turf, the heavenly scent of sea-campion clinging to the fissures of rock. Such pleasure was so very rare and she took in great gulps of air as if she hadn't breathed for years! The spring sun smoothed out her face; released the tension in her hands, lying palms up, now gently curled like opened shells.

The garden was, she remembered, a little inland, hidden from the sea spray which reached even this high on the winter winds, by a hedge of escallonia. The small gate was stiff catching on the rough path. Standing inside she could feel the weight of all the years of encouraging the herbs to grow out of the thin soil, yet it had been looked after somewhat. The paths were still visible and the hedge inside pruned back. Should her memory falter, she had only to follow the heady perfumes trapped here; the rosemary bush straggling in the far corner, the thyme and Origanum thriving in the heat.

When she had filled her pouch, it was time. Retracing her steps, she found the gate, and after a while, unerringly, the small dip in the cliff top. Here, pulling her cowl more closely around her head once more, she took the first precipitous steps down towards her cell and the call of the Angelus from the convent far below.

Turn Around

The lake lay like a silver platter in the corrie, etched with scalloped lines where ripples met the bright spears of the reeds, the rocky shore, the stunted rowan, the rough shingle.

Her sudden presence disturbed the air, so that the hand of the wind smoothed the reeds laying them flat for a moment. A flutter of wings, a raven's hoarse cry and all was again still.

By the side of the lake was the ice-carved stump of an old fallen tree where she now sat heavily and contemplated the expanse of muted, argent light. In winter this lake would quickly freeze and even now an unusual lack of movement gave the scene an eerie quality of waiting, like the moments before snow, and much later the long-awaited melting of the ice. The same impression was held in the boulders tumbled from the peaks, resting on the slopes in a curious kind of suspension and the scree looking impossibly steep, ready to slip with the slightest sound. All around the ancient mountains rose in timeless quiescence, unchanging forms against a waxen sky.

Being here – her startlingly red Parka and the unnerving restlessness within – seemed all at once a desecration. She had entered without due reverence and brought disturbance. So she sat still, trying to emulate the scene before her; to become unmoved, immovable.

Betrayal came in the agitated circling thoughts causing her to twitch, to itch to move, to get away, to forget through the escape of placing of one foot before the other on steep mountain paths, which required all one's concentration and brought, therefore, surcease. Compared with the tranquillity before her, her insides roared with 'sound and fury'. The words came up out of memory … 'signifying nothing' was how the stanza ended!

She bent forward until she could look at her reflection in the surface of the water. The impossible, impassable climbs out of the valley were reflected behind her pinched, trapped gaze, until the hand of the wind moved again, the image pixelated and scattered across the lake in rivulets of light. She became formless, floating, illusory.

To her left the bank had broken and the muddied shingle stretched path-like into the water. Still bending forwards, she removed her boots and let her coat fall behind her on the log. The pebbles were icy and slick under her feet, but walking into the grey water with the wet seeping up her trousers seemed the obvious thing to do. Even the wind now pushed against her back and it was easy to carefully place one foot before the other on the silted bed and feel the lake taking her into itself.

The suddenness of pink and gold before her was a shock like the firing of a gun. On the deadened steel of the surface the lily struck across her path as bold and fearsome a barrier as a rifle butt. In that abrupt awakening moment, she almost fell; stumbled, heart racing and in that automatic struggle for self-preservation found herself laughing out loud, the sound echoing off the mountain sides; reverberating like the ripples on the lake into the distance. That she should actually care about falling!

As her laughter died away so the fitful wind dropped again. The lake became once more silvered light, on the altar of which the lily audaciously, beautifully defied her.

And now, into the growing silence a small sound nagged at her … something so unexpected that she finally turned away from the deeper water and searched the mountainsides around. A faint call, or was it simply a bird … she found herself moving out of the cold, cold lake, all the while listening carefully for any further sound. And just as she reached the slippery shingle it came, unmistakably, a cry from somewhere on the mountain.

Hurriedly now she put on her boots and coat and almost ran in its direction. Leaving the corrie without a backward glance she clambered over rocks wet with rain and moss, slipping, stopping to listen, moving on, chasing the weak sound up and along the ridges, over the impossible scree and the bright streams which sprang down towards the lake from the high peaks above, creating caverns and gullies over which she leapt without thinking.

Breathing heavily, she eventually reached a huge boulder where she really had to climb, had to trust that there would be a handhold around the other side if she let go, but nothing would deter her now. The cries were closer, but getting weaker. So she leapt, her right hand reaching out like a claw as she did so, her feet striving to reach the narrow ledge on the far side. Having been so close to death there was no fear, only an urgency to find the source of that dwindling cry, as if it was an anchor for her own shifting consciousness.

And then she found it. Into a deep channel in the mountainside just in front of where her feet had landed, someone had fallen. He lay half-buried by the friable rock which had come down with him; the harness of his climbing gear tangled amongst the debris. He had obviously been there for some time, and in this remote place death from such a fall was almost inevitable.

'I'm here', she called down to him. 'You're safe. I have a phone.'

From out of the wreckage in the gully she caught the relief in his whispered reply: 'I heard you laugh'.

Sea Song

When the light fails and the shadows creep out across the stones, the night fishers slide over the seagrass shallows into the deeps. Bow waves stream smoothly, their crests catching the last rays like smoking fire. The sound of the engines fades into the distant indigo seas.

She listens until they are gone, sitting on the stone wall by the old men whose rheumy eyes gaze unseeing into the dusk, beads sliding through painful fingers that remember the pull of the nets, the slippery scales, the salt, salt sea.

She is invisible to them, her dark dress blending into the approaching night.

The fishers are gone and a hollow emptiness fills the warm air. One by one the old men move off down the hill towards the taverna, shuffling across the cobbles.

For a while all sounds stop. She floats on this timeless silent moment, feeling the ebb tide of thought flow beneath. She is weightless, formless, insubstantial; left behind in the stillness of the dark earth and sky, while the phosphorescence gleams in the far distance.

I am old, she thinks, I can no longer join the dancing in the square, be lifted by strong arms, feel the thrill of hope. I am old.

The smell of the sea drifts up the hill and envelops her ... so many memories carried in its seaweed tang, but they too flow on and are gone, hardly noticed.

She imagines the feel of the boat once more; the gently moving planks, the silent men, the breeze lifting their dark curls, the haunting sea song.

In the morning, as the golden light creeps up over the rim of the sea, and the boats sail back into harbour, they find Maria laying there, by the wall.

Hidden in the Wind

She lay hidden in the wind; curled into herself; into the small space which was unequivocally hers. She felt safe. Any sounds she might have made were flung away like leaves in autumn into the general stream of rushing, spinning air. The noise mercifully surrounded her more securely than any walls and in its continuous, pervasive hold, like a wild animal gone to ground, she slept.

She awoke with the light pricking her eyelids, just as the wind shivered into silence, acutely and immediately aware of the danger she was in. Now she would have to move and the thought drove sharp splinters of fear up from her belly to her heart. This space beneath the rhododendron thicket was dry; the dead leaves creating a pungent litter between the smooth old stems. To leave it felt the hardest thing she had had to do so far in this madness which now possessed her life.

She held her breath ... the soundless air was just as suddenly filled with a soft scrape of twigs and a sharp smell ... two bright eyes of wary fox stared into her, its haunches quivering with impending flight. She exhaled roughly and it was gone.

Now was the moment, yet still she hesitated, aware that visitors to her den could come in many forms, but subdued utterly by fear into a small bundle of aching stillness.

Outside the darkness was dissolving, grey wisps of day slanted in between the stems, curled into beckoning fingers to which she began, at last, to crawl. The woods were full of the dawn song. The spring morning a contradiction and a challenge to her feelings. Was she wrong to have run? Could she have misunderstood the coldness in the voice ... the sense of menace?

Bright sun lapped against her skin. Air perfumed with tree sap and all the myriad things which were beginning to grow, flowed around her ... filled her lungs. And then the unmistakable scent of tobacco. She stood and began to run ... ran as the fox must before the hounds ... ran like the wind racing in the night ... ran until the woods came to an end at the edge of ploughed fields.

And there they were coming towards her across the ruts, disturbing the young shoots, disturbing the morning with their shouts, calling her name. She was trapped, sides heaving from the run ... hardly able to understand. What were they saying? Her eyes blurred with tears. Mummy clasped her, hugged her fiercely: 'Thank God you're safe. We were rehearsing for a play my darling.'

Release

Bright rivulets chase each other down the sides of the steep lane after the storm. Crescents catching the light, released to flow to the lake in the dim valley below, trudged past wearily some fifteen minutes ago.

The pack he carries is heavy, but is light as the leaves which float down on the flood compared with the weight of what he holds in his mind. The wind whips up from the distant hills grey with cloud, carrying the sounds of traffic on the main road where he was dropped two hours ago. Ahead, the lane seems endless.

But eventually the top is reached and he stops. A solitary figure in the gathering dusk, leaning against the lichen-covered wooden post of the gate, resting his pack on the wet crossbar slippery from the rain. He looks at the familiar fields on either side. One ploughed and already sown with winter wheat. That will be Tom's: the persistence, the resilience of a good farmer. In the other the grey heads of cabbages ready to be harvested. Further down will be the sheep fields, grass-bitten and then the long paddock where Sally keeps her horses, and after that home … he can see the lights coming on in the gloom of the valley … they will be waiting. He will have to face it soon … the excitement, the noise and worst of all the questions …

He has to go on and hoisting the pack again, his feet sliding in the muddy grass, he stumbles downwards, the sky heavy overhead, until the horses come into sight. They are sidling up to the flint wall, ears erect, hearing the sounds of his boots on the tarmac coming down the hill – sensing the familiar in this stranger who appears out of the deepening shadows on a wet autumn night.

As he passes the paddock he walks on the rough verge near the wall trying to avoid the deeper water spilling across the lane from the sodden fields. The horses, bold now, try to nuzzle him, heads leaning over the stones searching for treats, one so enthusiastic that in a sudden movement the heavy weight of the pack pushed from the side throws him off balance and as it falls it spills its contents onto the grass, into the puddles. Frustrated he swears loudly, frightening the mare who veers away snorting. He scrabbles in the dirty wetness finding the torch in the side pocket, and scanning the ground in irritation for his things, gathering the soggy papers and objects randomly back into the pack, until one thing grasps his attention, the photo wallet, shoved out of sight until now. Almost forgotten … but not quite …

In the light of the torch it takes on significance, as if all else disappears into the murky night and the wallet – what it contains – is the only thing held in focus. He opens the wet leather leaves to see the colourful image staring up at him in the narrow beam. It shows a couple laughing, holding hands with a young boy, who stares out from between them full of uncomplicated happiness. Innocent and blameless. These words leap into his mind as he stares at his own young face, at the hands holding him safe, at the remembered love, and then, like a tide released from some distant shore he breaks … here in the gathering dark by the mossy wall, with the horses whiffling and munching in the paddock, the tears course as steadily and purposefully as the water tracks its way down the hills. All that they had tried so hard to get him to release in those hours of therapy now flowing, breaking over the muddy-thinking obstructions, carrying the past away: all that he had done and could not do.

Eventually the torrent of emotion ceases and he looks into the darkness towards his parents' farmhouse, with the lights now glistening brightly like stars in the aftermath of his tears, and shouldering his kit bag he walks down towards their joy; home, at last, from the war.

The Paintings

1.

'She was rescuing her dog. This is what she would say if anyone caught her trespassing', she thought, as she scrambled over the broken wall behind overgrown rhododendrons and found her way onto the meadow which once had been a lawn. The fact that there was no dog to be seen could make things more believable … at least for a while.

The truth was that she had seen the 'Arts and Crafts' style house from the path through the woods and was intrigued and mesmerised by the glimpses she caught, standing on tiptoe, of its run-down beauty. And having found the unexpected way in a little further on down the steep path, she now stood and scanned the peeling façade and the tangle of shrubs with an itch which only an artist could perhaps appreciate. 'A touch of Naples yellow here, and that wall is crying out for rose madder', her mind already composed the scene … but colour was her forté. Eventually, one solitary lighted window appeared out of the approaching dusk and she thought how sad and unloved it all seemed, and how beautiful it must once have been.

It was over a week before she could return, because return was inevitable … a pull so strong that she took all her paints, easel and stool, in the hopes that she would remain undisturbed and that the way in over the wall would not have been mended. 'This was very unlikely considering the state of the house and grounds', she thought. All was as before, the lighting perfect for what she wanted. So, perched amongst the old roses, to one side, but with a clear view of the moss-laden steps down from the back of the house, and the half-submerged dry fountain, she began. As often seemed to happen, it was as if the painting was just waiting for her to be focused, before it appeared out of the wings of her mind, fully-formed and ready for its audience. Brain became superfluous, hands and eyes had lives of their own and took off across the paper with lightness, fluidity and an intuitive understanding of what was required.

2.

The coffee was scalding hot and the sun beat fiercely into his eyes as he returned the cup to the café table. A feeling of complete ennui settled over him again like a shroud, despite the liveliness of the Italian morning. All around people laughed and talked, there was even someone singing nearby … Puccini perhaps … but what did it matter. The lethargy that had held him in its grip for several long months shut out the warmth of life, and left him with bitter dregs.

Yes, he was out and free … of sorts. Able to drink what he wanted, eat good food, be with women, but the memories of what he endured those months in prison and how he came to be there were mental and emotional bars as strong as any. Not only the guilt of his collusion with the tax swindle, but the eventual betrayal by his partner, clouded every moment. Feelings of shame would wash over him, so that to write became impossible. This Italian escape was an attempt to rekindle the innocent days before the fall and the magic of creativity he could conjure then, but a large part of him felt beyond redemption. The café filled with lunchtime noise and he left, to continue walking the quieter back streets of the old town without interest or purpose.

3.

No matter that the painting of the house was finished, still she felt herself drawn back to it, time and time again. Sometimes she would just sit or lie amongst the long grass and stare at the clouds, imagining the story behind the house's decline. Sometimes she would wake up out of a dream, where the house seemed to be calling to her ... a message passed on the winds of night from one deserted room to another. The obsessive nature of it frightened her, and one morning after a dream in which she walked the lonely rooms of the house calling plaintively ... she decided a holiday was called for ... a long holiday in an arid land, where desolate houses and overgrown gardens could be forgotten on the beach, in loud bars and lost under the sound of cicadas and summer music.

4.

The back streets of the town were full of a slightly sickly mixture of smells ... dogs, wisteria and spilled wine. Sometimes his senses would be awakened by the difference of it all ... by the cobbles when he tripped, by the bright bars of light and shade across the narrow roads between buildings and by the underlying smell of urine which reminded him to watch his step. Although not the haunts of tourists, still the enterprising Italians would open shops along these alleys and it was at one of these that he stopped, arrested by the paintings in the window. It seemed odd to find them here, and even more so when one picture drew his eye in astonishment. It was his house and garden, but not as he'd left it months ago. Everything about his home had been brought back to life ... the colours so pulsating that he could see why it would sell in this Mediterranean country, where nature and paintwork were vibrant with life. How could someone have done this! ... the house so unusual that it could not have been painted by coincidence? How did they get in? He found himself inside the shop without realising it, studying the painting's details. The fountain (working), the pitched and gabled roof, the roses trained against the old walls. He searched for a name at the bottom, but could only find the initials RM. The shopkeeper from whom he bought the painting (of course) at an extortionate price, even for something so beautiful, had no idea who the artist was. And it seemed he couldn't remember how he came by it ... which they both thought was odd ... maybe a fault of the language difficulties, but still ...

Back in his room, with the painting propped against the wall and lying on the white cover on the bed, he couldn't stop gazing at it. Everything about the house and gardens had been transformed, indeed reversed, as if the artist had known how it used to look. The feeling it engendered in him was like surfacing from a deeply troubled sleep to find the sun melting away the phantoms and rekindling the fragrance of new growth, of flowers and cut grass, of scented roses in the first flush of summer. It gave him back his life. This sounded dramatic in his head, but was the truth nonetheless. He felt young again, unsullied by the immediate past and ready for the next step ... which was to go home he realised all at once; to go back to that house and make it happen, return it to its former loveliness like the painting.

The next weeks are a whirlwind of activity back at the house. With the help of friends and contractors everything is renewed and rebuilt. The garden is rediscovered, and the roses blooming against the cleared wall, fill the air with sweetness. He is writing again, filling his days with hard work and his evenings with creative thoughts which spill onto the page flowing from his mind and fingers (he must get a laptop) like a rainstorm ... the paper soaking up the ink like a desert landscape under the welcome storm. And at weekends, when he feels he can leave his writing safe to return to, he scours the local and London galleries (he really must get a computer), for anymore of the artist's distinctive work. The painting has a prominent place on the wall at the end of his bed, and is a reminder of the dark place he's been and the possibility of transcendence ... of rediscovering wholeness at any moment.

The first time he found a painting by the same artist he was thrilled, but the name still escaped him. Apparently they wished to be as anonymous as possible ... something to do with being scarred by criticism in the past, he discovered from a dealer sympathetic to his quest, but he would not, or could not tell him more. After that second find, he bought several more of the artist's works and displayed them all around his house ... their brightness singing in each room. He studied them so often, in a relaxed and non-professional way, that he felt he began to understand the driving need behind the artist's style ... always an element of bringing something to life, of instilling colour and energy, infusing the pictures with hope.

5.

After a time, the pleasures of the world tend to cloy, no matter how enjoyable they are. The dreams of the house had receded, and thoughts turned to her studio at home. She had amassed a huge number of studies of local life; of seascapes, tree-lined promenades and mountain vistas hazily receding into the distance, and it was time to give them colour and life.

Back in the cool, north-facing room in the village house she rented, she worked with all the passion of that hot country she had left ... as if the muscles of her hands and the cells in her mind had stored all the sun and were now pouring it out in colours which scintillated and leapt off the canvas. One of her usual gallery owners, over a glass of Chianti, was stunned into unusual silence, out of which came the words in his strong French accent: 'You must exhibit! This I will arrange. Do not argue, ma petite, these must be shown.'

6.

The excitement he felt when the gallery owner contacted him was extraordinary, and yet perhaps not surprising considering how much had changed in him, and 'Oui, monsieur, the artist would be there'. The opening night was invitation only, but after that the artist would be in residence, he felt sure.

7.

After the commotion of the opening night in the gallery, the photos, the chatter, the explanations, not to mention the exhausting amount of work to get everything ready, she was drained. The following morning lassitude overtook her to the degree that she phoned the gallery and, claiming a bad headache as the result of too much champagne, she cried off being there for that day, and yes, she would come in for the rest of the week, she promised dear Henri.

Having made these excuses, suddenly she wanted to be out of the studio and in the sunshine ... away from crowds and alone with the cool calm of the trees and the grass, with the sky and the wind. Inevitably, it seemed, her mind returned, now it was free to do so, to the house in the woods ... to the beginning of this journey. It couldn't hurt to visit just one more time ... to lie in the grass and smell the scents of lush foliage.

All the way there, she couldn't quite believe the excitement of returning. The path through the woods was calming, sunlight dappling the ground as she walked. She came to the wall, and yes, it was still broken. But the sight which greeted her on the other side of the dense bushes, was so unexpected she was transfixed with one foot on the cut grass of the lawn and one in mid-air. It was her painting come to life ... lived in front of her ...

and as she walked further across the lawn the strangest feeling was of stepping into one of her own pictures … like a weird Dali moment. The fountain dropped precious coolness into the oval pool beneath, the steps up to the house were filled in nooks and crannies down the sides with scented herbs and the house itself was freshly painted with, yes, something in places like Naples yellow!

8.

The disappointment he felt when the artist did not appear in the gallery the day after the opening night was out of all proportion. No matter that the owner, Henri, promised the artist would be there the next day and for the rest of the week. He had been full of questions and now they would have to wait yet another day. Still, what he saw as he eventually began to stroll around the gallery, was compensation in itself and transported him, once again, out of melancholy into joy. How this artist managed to achieve such shifts in people's consciousness was a skill he admired deeply and with awe. He only hoped that some of the skills were transferrable through his observation to his own art form … to be able to do this for his readers was something to aim for with all one's soul.

After an hour or two of being lost in the artist's unique world, he left the gallery full of inspiring thoughts, which streamed from mind to paper (a laptop was a must now) as the train carried him out of the busy city and home. And yes, another oblong package travelled with him. This one he thought would go well in the conservatory overlooking the garden, its colours mirroring the richness of the late summer flowers.

9.

She aroused from a dreamy languor with a smile. A cloud had covered the sun and the change in light had opened her artist's eyes fully. 'How did you get in here?' said the cloud, who was in fact a man bending over her. Startled she stumbled upright, brushing down her skirt unnecessarily, to gain composure. 'Well?' the rising inflection of his voice summoned her mind back from its sleepiness completely.

'Over the broken wall', she managed to say, pointing in the direction of the bushes at the edge of the lawn. 'What broken wall?' he said, 'Every one of them has been repaired since I got back'. This necessitated a trip to the bushes, an inspection of the wall and several very strange sideways glances in her direction from the man, who must, she realised be the owner. 'Oh lord!'

All at once he seemed to come to a conclusion about something. Her eye, used to the subtleties of nuance and shade, caught a moment when something changed in him, as if the sun had revealed a secret ... and it had nothing to do with the wall. 'Come', he said, 'It's time we had some tea'. And it seemed as natural as anything to go with him. Now that the storm of him finding her was over, there was a compulsion of quite another kind which led her in his footsteps up those lovely scented steps into the conservatory and into the shock of her life ... for there on the wall opposite the garden was a painting from her exhibition … and into the silence of recognition came a plaintive question, which contained all the longing of the lost and the reunion of the found, 'What is your name?'. Hearing the sound of his voice, she turned and smiled into her future, 'Rose Madder', she replied.

Falling Stars

There is light in the winging dark. An ebony cloth is laid over the sky and the hand of God sprinkles the stars into its hollows and folds. One of these faint lights is our beginning. It consumes the space behind us, growing larger with our memories and in its dying. Another is just a glimmer ahead, not even a light as yet, merely a place of aspiration; the arrow's point before it arrives.

We take it in turns to be awake, a few years at a time, to watch the gasses in the nebulae shoot their vivid colours into the void; their names now meaningless, will there be crabs and horses where we will live? Interstellar dust has no such warmth.

Then one time we are all awake. The computers tell us that we must prepare for gravity again, for other skies and the return of life. A star hangs behind us and we are hurtling inward to encircle another blue-green planet.

Our probes find soil and sea, landscapes with what seem to be plants, rocks, trees, recognisable, yet with an otherness which is strange in its familiarity.

Leaving the big ship, we descend into our new lives; step onto this earth under a different sun. This first night we stand together under the night sky, while the stars, falling all around, silently envelop the world.